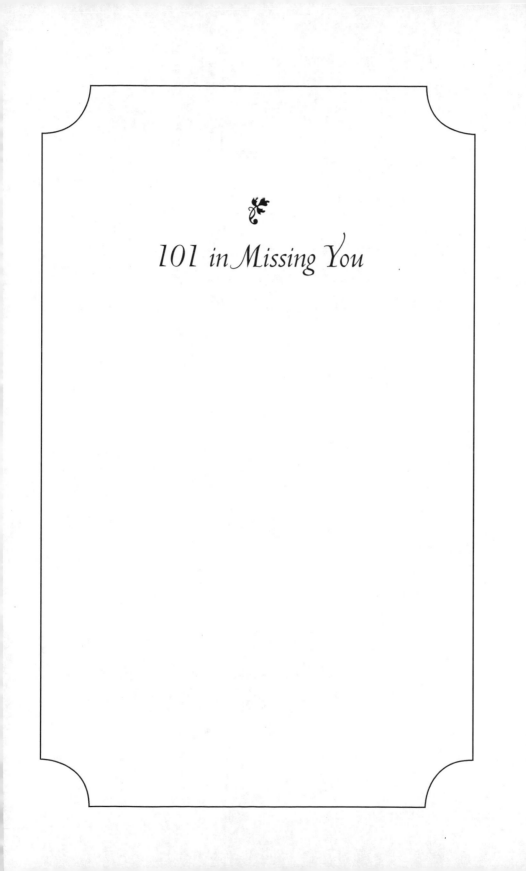

101 in Missing You

101 in Missing You

Sarah Patricia Condor

iUniverse, Inc.
New York   Bloomington

101 in Missing You

iUniverse books may be ordered through booksellers or by contacting:

iUniverse
1663 Liberty Drive
Bloomington, IN 47403
www.iuniverse.com
1-800-Authors (1-800-288-4677)

ISBN: 978-1-4502-0972-4 (pbk)
ISBN: 978-1-4502-0973-1 (ebk)

Printed in the United States of America

iUniverse rev. date: 2/5/2010

Contents

To the one who taught me how to love.

101 in Missing You

"I miss you..." What a platitude!
One cannot say it without being rude
Things everyone says every day
Like: "I wish that I could stay"
"I wish I'd never have to go..."
And "I love you – love you so..."

Some mutter "love" over a glass of gin
Spitting, snarling: "Where you bin?"
Others on the telephone, remain content
All alone, all in their element
While others still seek but know not what
Conquistadores spelling "gold" for God

Someone out there says it all the time
For him or her I would not give a dime
One who misses everybody, more or less,
Needs but ThemSelves for happiness
Truly happy with a TV and a chip
Lest their lives should falter, fall or slip

My own missing is a Missing 101
I had but a crash course, like a nun
Or, rather, like a duchess growing old
Longing for a steady arm to have and hold
Longing for your smile, your kind word
How you fight, how you wield your sword

Missing and missing and missing you
Even a phone call now would do
Staring through the window pane
Walking with my eyes closed in the rain

Seeing you down the alley by the park
I would blow my kisses to the parting bark

I would wait until the seas grow calm
And pray that you come to no harm
I would write and sing and dream
And meet you in between the lines
In a spell-bound book of crimes
In a most thrilling book of schemes

That is to say, I speak no platitude
When I repeat: I miss the Prince the Brute
The Knight, the General, and the Captain too
All those men that spell like Y-O-U…
I had a "101" in missing as you know
So I see you – see you still – everywhere you go.

Each Time You Go Away

It is a cloudy, rainy day, and I
Do not have much to say
But spell your name in my Heart
And hope that you will return

But then – when did we ever part?
You may have your road, your way
Your resolutions, words to say
Much ahead – and much astern…

And I too have my role to play
Home to cherish, warm, and stay
Our little garden, dog, and yard
Our flowering roses, Fichus, fern…

At times, each a solitary bard
At other times all joyful – come what may!
We sail together – here, and far away
With Huck on the raft we yearn…

Or conjure up our big white whale
While the day palely passes by
And the Fires of the Heart strike the sky
Vivid and wild they burn, they burn

They bring you back – I pray
Each time I see you go away…

A Footstep to Appall

There was a buzz upon my window pane
There was a footstep in the unseen snow
That freshly fallen on the backroads of my mind
Was thawing with the rattle of the wheels

I dreamt a dream: a dale of daisies vain
Unveiled and asking where was I to go
Where was this road to end, this wheel to wind
Where was I to fall, to rise again, to kneel

To pray to the fly upon my crazy brain
To fly with the soldier-flakes – row-by-row
Final the fight – too cruel to be kind
To let myself let go, let go of what was real?

How was I to know? To tell I am too plain
Too little awake am I, and much too slow
To find out before my time – to find
Beyond the momentary buzz: what fills the air?

What is and is not there as I arise to fall
A flake of thawing snow upon your mind
A call from the Great Beyond, a footstep to appall…

Where Spirits Sway

Sometimes, after dark,
When the crowns of the trees are swathed in softly descending night,
Images appear, shadows loom ahead, and you path
Alive with spirits, whispers: we-we-we
We were here, we are here, are true...

And you wish to touch them
Shadows of the night, you speak to them in a constrained tenor, asking:
Why? – no response... But
If it were not for the darkness, which has filled the air
You would wipe off a dewdrop in your eye...

We are all human, all human as we are
We cry at times, and know not why; and then – women, men – ashamed
Look up in the sky and see
How those shadows fit in with our Selves – as silently we pass
Strolling at random in the grass...

Now on the steady earth, now as if we walked on water
Others have cried here long ago – or not so long? – Who can tell? Who
can know
What ailments of beatitude may bring
A winding path of shadows that will sway and swing and speak
Ever so softly to your ear:

We were here, we are here with you
Tonight is tomorrow is –
Or is not true?

Thank You

I can never thank you enough
for my first celebration of love
of real life which is equally mani-
fold and never burns at both ends
either (just as those little candles)
burns fast yet – silence comprehends
and we (or me rather) cannot wait
for the best always to come and
after you shall have taken yours
then like a surreptitious squirrel
I will munch mine only to fill the cup
and run away from one conscience
to another along the path the
mountain made for me – you dear
cannot crack nuts and so this day
let me thank you and say – as long
as the solid down deep stays unspent
you lend me your machete and as long
as you trust my judgment then I
shall firstness lastness make and today
make last the first and last and
crack nuts for us till heavens burst
words do not rhyme and the melody
sung on occasions such as these
unbreak even my loving kiss
on your scorching lips my unsure
unveiled unforgiving weeps for some
secrets even the squirrel could not tell-
(many things might fell the mountain –
gales, earthquakes, too much rain or none
at all...) so I should stay a small squirrel
even on top of you – true enough but

there are no nuts there and rough
weather and the first may become last –
I am not perfect: past song and play
say many a nut I left uncracked too
I only thank you for everything my love
Unbeing 31: – more nuts? – more you?
– more true? – before we grow old
will you teach me how to sing? and
thank you   also for the golden ring.

Your Queen

an egyptian
queen
star of byzantine spaces roaming
shedding leaves
grieves for
more graces
places in the sun
(perhaps everyone does so?)
past – slow – and – gone
(where did it go?)
i am the last
have no sword to bury
in avalon
have no albatross to nail
to the mast
have no laurels of sin
yet i am
your queen

Before You Came By

I was kissed by a beast at birth
Blessed with Spring Infuriations
Midnight remembrances and
Melancholy of subsiding memories

I was plucking the plumes of pain
Then again (after an Ishmael came)
Enciente with Anatomies of Summer
Kissed as a Venus in furs

I was – not as I should have been
Beseted by my own dreams and
Aboulia – deletritus – Dante's Fire
Sire: I acquired the taste for *introits*

But I was *de rigeur* and – Dana?
You remember Dana the Irish
Witch who used to teach me more
Insane and sore and scortatory

Ways of arrested wills: I was
Out of tune – *adagio* – unfulfilled
A Movement in a Rock was I
Before – My Love – You came by.

Home

I lost many a home in my life
Or what I thought of as –
Homes? Houses? Happiness?
With a sink, phone line, and a lover
Sometimes the looks of the Fortune cover
Empty as a shop-window, a T.V. screen
Mannequins of may-have-been…

Lingering by, muted, forgotten now
Each in the shadow of his rotten vow
Behind a smudged window-pane
Pleasure come–gone, some pain…

No, I have stopped counting sheep
And only sometimes do I see
Those houses, places, empty faces
Homeless now, remembering me…

I have some vices, and some graces
I am no holy cow
I am too simple for too many places
For me, home is only one, and
I am done counting now –
Home is what the Heart embraces.

I

You make me write strange poetry
You make me say weird things
Tie laces on a desert tree
Establish funny links

Say "I believe" because I love
And love because I am
Scream "more!" where just "enough"
Would sound much better – damn!

Is this I or just a flea
Born – reborn – on the brink
Of the blue – bottomless – the sea
The sea, where the flea will sink?

I say weird things again
Like it is painful just *to be*
Like pleasure equals pain
And pain is pleasure inside me

But I know not what I say
I am Beatitudes of Love
I am a word in your Play
But to memorize me?
– that is tough.

Thinking of You

I wrote this poem in late afternoon
solitary, in a swoon
thinking of you
dozing off
fading –

I wrote this poem in hope of you
trading a few words and
looks and touches
of loneliness
of love –

I wrote this poem to bless the day
that it flies so quickly by
that soon you and I
will be us
again –

From
Ode to My Man

I groped in Baghdad for Scheherazade's lore
I craved for better letters – more ink?
Persephone's fate was not mine too
Late I discovered *boites-de-nuit*
See – been there before but never realized
How oversized Camus' Sisyphus is
Or what I missed so much – no
Hiss and hush of the curtain call…

I craved for – ? More hope less praying
A renegade and sacrilegious beast
A witch – in feast on the low God
Brings me nothing: I believe not in
Nothing Miss Nobody – no solace no cure no
Prey – pray and move – sitting duck
Ink for you my love – the proof
Of all my earthly doings

In-deed the second best is the light
I might even glimpse some seraphim or
Swim cross the Styx (or the Rubicon
for that matter) I wrought my Will
To suit your eyes… better still
I drowned in the Paradise of your voice
Did I have a choice? Reverberating
Stating desire and lifelong dreams

Seems I can sing with you and efface
The ineffable – spaces – echos – eyes –
Sieve and touch you grain by grain

One by one until the deed is done not
In words and letters or in verse but
In the language of the Universe
I feel (and feel I can):
You are my Love – my Man.

Dreams

Again and again: I do
Am going too
Do those – things

I flog and slap them
Torture and torment
Wring and twist

Cause agony
Me – Me – ever so meek now
Make them see

Squirm and struggle
Tumble and steam
Torpid whims

Then listless, low:
Where did you go?
I hate you so…!

Cureless

The beads of sweat on your forehead
The heat of breath and wink of eye
A summer lullaby of azure and red in the sky
Of unheard cries and unseen faces...

My soul braces against the falling dark
Forlorn and far like a Beaudelaire's bark
The past growing thin along the edges
Wedged among Donatello's swaying saints

Engraved and craved and saved for later
Alligator tears and fears to be
Imported uninsured from another century
Dutch pottery or a Greek urn on a lark

Searching for more after – after dark
The teacup the myrrh and labdanum
In a metaphysics saturated room
I abjure, I abdicate – I adjudicate:

Is it too late to procure for tomorrow?
Amour and sorrow – bead by bead
Not fit for a fallen hero's head
But – for a fighter who shall last
      Until the light returns: mad for the light!
      Mad! And yet, she yearns and yearns...

Marrow of Being Me

My Soul, a disheveled lilac
The color of roses sprung too soon
Pink but to *verdâtre* tinged

I talk to myself: *Ma petite*
The Other Me, she supposes
That all things can be seen –

That all descent and rise
The tingle in the ear
The Sirens' call so near, so near

A Soul behind the veil
Continents – out there for to sail!
The Will mesmerized the Mind –

Wild within while without
She wonders still…
The Marrow of Being

> Inside the *Other Me*
> No other me can kill.

Call You Now

I wish I could call you
To say that I shall burst or
Overflow, any minute now
With the power so true
So glaring and so gore…

I must call you now!

To hear the voice that I adore
Tingle for, and meow
In red, in yellow, and in blue
Daisy petals soar: I
Wisp and winnow on your brow

If only you would call me now…

If only to hang up and restore
The silent solemn vow
We gave each other – no review
Nothing really bargained for
At the time – not here and now!

If only I could call you now!

Huntington Library

Spruces and pines and vines of reason
Seasonless insecure impassioned: we
Grow at the sight – and sigh and smile
In silence soft to guile a squirrel
Who comes to pay a visit from her tree

All at ease, committed to treason
As if we for seeing could not see
The memory of the Blue Boy and the bile
Like faded murals from Venice-Italy
Miles for Danae – Leda – Oh, shortsighted me!

Elysian lawns in late afternoon sun
Round tables chairs and effigies
We stroll through aisles of history
Hand in hand and heart to heart
You and I in the sea of magic art.

Father's Day

I wish I could give you more
On this, your Father's Day. In fact
Only now do I begin to understand
Cordelia – what she really meant…

I blame not Lear but do recall instead
All the adventures we have always had:
A few hundred days: one library
One museum, theatre, one supper…

No Tupperware parties or week-ends
But no lose ones neither – together
Ever so happy (apart from one gale
A few words and a few other people…)

Some memories should rot – go stale
For we shall never fail to recall
All of it – even the sorry part, and spit
Out the aftertaste of pain…

Because this is for real once again
This cup can never fill too much
For such is Love: stock-still secure
And pure for the naked eye – yet

Madly rushing around the orb
Eager to die or absorb all universe
When one word or verse fails…
(Different in mail – remember?)

The page, still largely pale, stares back:
Lack words? Lack of props or etiquette?
What is the norm and customary?
To pay for dinner, drink some wine…

To forget about a kiss upon a cheek I miss
Your touch so much… your Love
The Brittle Thing, in between us
No walls to be mended and

Flowers watered to the very end…
No magic wand – no mobile phone
All alone I think of you while you
Remain true and keep your word…

Here goes your everything – I hope –
I grope no more in darkness deep
And bless the world by us
To sleep in peace, orbiting the sun

Day and night, year by year
Apart-together, always here, for
All days are holy – let us celebrate
For Cordelia, Lear… it is much too late

In us Love can create – or recreate
Or else, most certainly, will kill.

Yet Unbegotten

The light in the frontyard tells me NO
You will not go this way Tonight
Not tonight – like every other day:
Out of Sight is out of Mind they say
Should I add: out of Heart?

Let me start again – this time
In rhyme with what should be
For as I assigned my Me to You
I do my due by this Decree
Sacredly signed in Honesty:

This War with the Self called *amour*
A cureless disease we must endure
No reassurance come what may
In Tomorrow is of Yesterday
Let us pray for – what is *vorbotten*

Me – *du machst* – unbegotten Me
I toss and turn and think of Destiny
Craving for you… to put out the light
The day still in sight, forgotten Me
I sigh and greet another forlorn night

In falling asleep I go – I pass through the gate
I follow Thee – I call it Fate.

Exhortations

Done in Her Eden for Fools
Cruel-less, mirthful, Falstaff-like
Some spike to it, some wit?
Not enough to call it Love.
What then is the goal? Survival?

How about the Soul? We aspire
Like dough upon a heated stove
With a drop of that sacred Leaven
Remnants in the after-rain dew
Mauve, dizzy, dandelion streaked

Faint and meek, as if on canvass drawn
Sawn in the history of the Heart
Recoiling, wishing to start anew
Kiss me! Kiss… as I kiss You…
With a plea and a prayer for more

More Time drowned in your disheveled hair
More rhyme, more strophe of caress
With a blessing on your lip
With more chances for to bless
Till dawn, and then on and on

Until another day should die
And the Night come back
                    to certify our Love.

Apple of Rebirth

I am a lonely apple tree:
One apple and one worm
Torn between the Soil
And recoiling Heavens
Toiling till sunrise then –
Revert from men.

Me within Me – the Demise of Being
Still fleeing to be – still
On the run…

The story has no end
To comprehend go pluck
The Apple – suck the Worm
Grapple with the Storm
Be reborn as a Tree
Be born again – like Me.

why

rain smears memories... roses
bow their heads but do not cry

only sigh: this Galahad in love...
enough! too brief is life!

be brave! they wink and sigh
again: no pain of might-have-beens

sinful dreams and denials and
trials of passing prayers

in tiers in layers rent
between lullabies

in the nectarines you glean
on your rose-less the queen

i shall not ask – i will not cry
i cannot tell you why

Moon by Me

I watch the Moon go down on me
Like so many times before
She swirls my Self in the Sea
So thin and cold and blue
I am She – and who are you?

Old and wise, comforting Moon
She cannot pale nor lose her hue
Grow stale, dispirited, in swoon
Or wrinkle in the face of time
Faint in the shadow of a rhyme...

Parsec by parsec, never apart
Unbroken – revolving – history
She is Me and I am in your Heart
Mirror of Destiny to sailors like You
Promontory – a lighthouse true

You see, I would never invite You here
To lie by my fragrant shade –
Never would I utter, my dear
This Prophecy of Becoming, being To Be
If it were not for the Moon going down on me...

Do Not Despair

Do not despair for Want of Love
At times, Life is not kind –
Cruel wind doth blind us –
Rocks will try to burst the Heart…

Is it the danger of the Start?
Flying too close to the Sun?
Trying the Wind on the run?
Above the stormy seas of Life?

It is what makes or breaks us is this Strife
Who we are – and will remain
Some, of stardust made, and pain
Crave those above that star-to-star in…

See: True Love is never truly far –
A sigh, despair, a silent prayer
Makes the wind, the rock – much fairer

Do not despair for want of Love
Those stars will shine upon your way
Stardust is the fare to pay for Truth

We all have paid our due
Before we learned to say: "I Love"
I Love Thee True.

Spelling LOVE

There are many ways to spell
Each and every simple word
Backward and front as you heard it
Or upside down, as no-one did

Or textbook-bound, as seems fit
To connect the ends together
Or line-by-line to make them never end…

It fails me now, I cannot comprehend
The Power of a simple word
Hours have passed since I heard it

So I vainly spell it out: El-oh-we…
E? "E" for Eternally…
Even "Destiny" comes with a "Y"

Why? There was a little bird one day
Came by your window, spelling *vai* and *we*
She came to stay, to learn to spell

The Spell of L-O-V and E in
Everything that was, that is, and is to be.

before winter sets in

before winter sets in
we shall begin

obtain what is necessary
to carry out our charge
with pride –

we confide in trecs
we tell the mountains
about our fight –

about the people who
will never give in –
who fight to win!

before winter sets in
we shall begin...

But for My Dreams

I take a stroll through silent night
I might resemble the other me –
Sarah Woodruff – Molly Bloom
Exhaled out of history – the Doom?
Preordained swoon of poetic flight
From Me to me –
                Nothing went quite right…
You see: there could be Light now
You could be here by my sight
With pride facing the Last Night
When whatever dies in these tears
Would rise again in your kiss
Like this – (a stroke of hand)
                Innocent as strawberries
I cherish the pastels of your Eye –
May I sing a lullaby? – the dying kind?
My wings shed tears… Find me! Find Me
Fearlessly stepping out of dark
And back – no sound left behind
But me – (and my dreams)
                Silence that Screams:
Mindless –
But for my dreams
Dreams about Thee…

Early hours' desperations

Early hours' desperations
Conversations in between
Myself and the Other Me
Over Destiny and the sin
Of Disobedience

Hence the conclusion rises:
Small paradises for little
People of brittle ways
While the Other stays silent
Untrammeled un-rent un-

Done in Her Eden for Fools
Cruelless – mirthful – Falstaff-like
No spike – but not enough
To call it Love. Survival?
Perchance revival of the lost

Soul? We aspire to Heaven
Rise like leaven in dough
In a heated stove – slow but
Fit and deadly effective too
True love? After-rain mauve

Color of Dandelions fainted
Canvassed – painted in oil
Recoiling above like puffs
Of snuffing sexagenarians
Bemoaning arias of Puccini's

Kiss me! Kiss... the Little Me
(You see I could not be one)
Shall plea and implore for
More and more and – Time
Trickles... Pour you Devil!

Disheveled hair and rhyme
The crime is over and you
Enter – true again in dawn
And Time has one Little Me
And my Destiny is yet to be.

Things You Do Not Know

There are things you do not know
Tiny and trifling they may seem
But they mean everything to me

See – the frown of your bushy brow
Throwing emotions at me now
Then in a silent swoon you meditate

Over a drink, some amiable memory…
The beauty in your naked eye that be
Forever piercing through my very Heart

I bleed. I blight the weakest Part of me
I spell *To Be* in a late night cup of tea
Reflected, wringing inside me is –

You! Eternal Happiness, I scream in between
The distant sighs drowned in a summer's rain
I should think I am much too vain

To say you are my Future and I am yours
So I surrender to the course of *l'amour*
I faint, but fearless by your side… *toujour*

Your breaths – what music to my Ear
Please, stay – if it were but in a dream, stay!
Behold! Let us breathe together, pray –

Let us inhale eternity tonight –
Let us thank the stars for this delight –
Let us never ever die!

I cry? I cry! It is for joy I cry
For small sounds, for unseen touch
For a word that means so much

That it can cut and tear and rend
Yet heal at the same time and then
Leave me longing for You, my Man…

Oh, for Heaven's Sake! I can never get enough
Of little things which make – Great Love.

In Your Eye

In your Eye I spy my Heart
Thou art nearer than a thought of Thee
In me – here

I fear... I am blind
I cannot see for Love –

Being reborn in your Eye
Reborn in Love
Until I die.

Sleeping Beauty

Sleeping Beauty has a duty
The Duty to arise: Up! Alas!
Sleeping cutie sleep no more
You! You have a duty call!

The Duty calls but Beauty sleeps
No promises she ever keeps
Deep is a pit-fall is her sleep
Sleep before – and after? Sleep.

Wrens and jays a-chirp and yell
Who put Thee in a sleeping spell?
There is a whole World out there
Sleeping Beauty, won't you care?

The Beauty turned, a smile to spare
She winked at you through her hair
Then fell deeper into sleep –
Waiting for her prince's kiss

Will you come, and count her sheep?
Will you come, and will not miss?

In Green

Distilled evening air – chilling
Memories – rimes, recollections
Thrilling – waiting like this –
Vienna Blood – Strauss' reflections
I can see you coming near – I
Fear what you cannot feel:

The air distilled – the chill – the rime
Time and spaces passing by… aye
Am I your Lady-in-waiting?
Meditating Mermaid yet to be?
Swaying by the gate – by the trunk of a tree…

It is getting late – I can see
You so close to me that I reach out
And all is green and all is blue – your eyes, your hair
Your face and smile and kiss…
All of you – my Happiness!

The stars above your head – the Moon
Green-blue silver late-night swoon
All is the hue of memory – I swoon, I gleam
I blossom here alone in blue and green
Distilled in the dye of Dream.

Silence

I arise to the hums and noises of a silent room
Silence greets me with regret
Silence – an old lady with dry, wrinkled cheeks
Silence – the eye of the meek meeting God
This is not the silence of the room in which I slept
This is not the quietude of a child that wept enough
For a fancy of a fairy-tale of love and fulfillment
Silence that would have meant to comfort me

What it is, is the silence of eternal longing
The silence of regret and a passing memory
Upon a regretful pause, after the memory has spoken
The remembrance that shall assail and persevere
As it returns in a hum – unbroken –
Harrowing, horrible, humid and molding
Coming to pester and flail, to harass and hold
A humble human soul under its spell

What it is, is the silence returning to assail
A dog once harassed – abused by an unknown hand
Now turning its eyes up upon you and me
In silent reproach – with a simple inquiry
In passing silence – now twice shy with a softer bark
For, somehow, only the beast can understand
The works of the deeper human mind
More palpable than a naked hand

Pray, how is Silence done by you?
Stillness? Nothing to speak of, live for, to exist?
Silence that twists all meanings into death
With nothing left in-between...
Silence that sits upon empty chairs
Silent audience that stares you in the eye
And before it should perish, it should die
Unseen, grasped and noticed by you – becomes yours

My silence is not the silence of the desert
Deep at night, the silence of the distant moon,
The graveyard silence of a five-year-old
That longed for but his mummy's hold
It is but a drape upon dreams and resolutions
Silent thickness spread upon a Versailles gallery
Reveries of palaces and domes – a painted tree
In solutions of the painter's manic chemistry

It is a Religion and Faith that struggles till the last
That cannot be until the very Silence screams
Upon awakening, in echos of our dreams
Out of a cave where silences like shadows cast
Chiaroscuro hopes on a wall of stone – long, lasting
Pass by us, crawling in recognitions, imprinted in stone
Rocked by the night that binds us all alone –
Where is the spotlight, the fifteen-minute Fame?

Instead, some virtuoso parrot in the audience
Cracks a joke and a few more people laugh at us...
Silence disappears, emulsion of thick air
Stuffed into the fissures and crevices of ancient walls
Or as hundreds of small silent spaces, silence calls
Forming circles in the air – halos crowning the Past
Reverberating in lonesome longing minds
Glorioles of wreaths, insubstantial whiffs of odor

What it is, is the sound of space as up we leap
As sparrows stepping on one another's nests
Waking up to our own silent calls
Greeted by the hum of regrets and recollections
Sensations that we learn to know – to accept
Longing for more – silence, as before
Untold tales and unheard melodies, dreams
Dreams, eternal silences that we cannot not keep

And we wish to scream – to disturb the universe
Like many before, and many after us will do
To stuff the moment with Love and Light
Like the rays of sunshine on a bookshelf as we wake up
To descry the dust of our illuminated souls and hearts
To wake the dead to sing along, to sing of silences
Of the pounding of the seas within, the throbbing wind
The years that run like rabbits in the Spring
To sing, to sing, to wake up and sing…

A Swan Dream

She is a swan upon the calmest of lakes
Disappearing in the distance only to return
In another form, so much nearer by your side…

While people pass us by, their eyes
Blank oysters in your plate
They give you a nod: it is getting late…

Perhaps, they are just longing for your dream
Of whipped cream of stars and galaxies
Floats of Love and Blessed reveries…

People are always like something else
With tentacles and textured skin
Lizards longing for more warmth and green…

Wayward afternoons wander into foreign lands
And people come and go – migrating swallows
Horizon-to-horizon, love-and-hate…

Looking for mates on the fly, because
The end does not die out there but within
Where it all began, where it must begin again…

In recoiling undercurrents in her wake
As she strains her neck to look stately, look at you
And we both stare for eons eye-to-eye…

And the clouds pass by like oversized Mesozoic reptiles
And the sailors feast on lobsters and prawns of the Permian age
And no-one contemplates the end…

Never linking the likenesses of magnitudes
Until one day just before dawn
There she comes, the swan that casts all spells…

Everyone can see her, but no-one tells the tale
Because a new day arrives, sunshine takes you on
And the stars grow pale in the light of day –

A swan sails by, and you can read in her eye:
Life is just a play, the lake is calm and deep
Tomorrow we will fly, but not today
Today we must stay our being free.

Angels

Angels thrown in a drift of snow
One by one, with no place to go
Under the stare of a wise old crow
Only she and the sky did know
Two happy angels in the snow
One Winter – years and years ago...

Night of Love

A halo of stars
Falling from above –
A Night of Love

Innumerable suns
Dreams of colors, shades
The Moon, the Fates –

The growing Moon
The stars falling close
A twitch of your nose –

Eternity in a kiss
Scented hair in summer breeze
Hold her, keep her, seize

Tonight, firm as ever,
For it may never end
If you will understand

A halo of stars
Falling from above –
Tonight, Night of Love.

Waiting for your call

I shall pass by the road unseen
Imagine places I have never been
Myself up upon the Milky Way
And pray for Thee to stay to stay...
I shall fly aloft and float above
Disclose to sleepers all my love
Uncover heavens in one sight
Set all wrongs right and then – ?
Cry some more – cry for my Man
If she can – so can I
Miss Eternity and Mrs. Lullaby...

Converted

I am a converted Jew, said the girl on the news
How about you? Would you fancy some more – ?
She smiled, a polite, courtroom smile
Saying that she ran away, and did it in style…

I too ran once, long ago, I ran away from home
Wanted to find out if all roads lead to Rome
Play catch-me-if-you-can awhile
Always going for it – mile-for-mile…

Like years ago, I am tempted, now, to leave
Ask me why – nothing else to give
As a cow on a Swiss turf chewing weed
It is high time to withdraw, to recede…

I am too old to run but I can saunter still
As I always have: with Pride, and Heart, and Will
I am wholly unfit for this enterprise
Like that girl on the screen, unsought Paradise…

But as for you, please, stay behind
Life is a great Play, and you are such a mastermind!
With a card or two up your sleeve
Everybody can convert, everybody can believe…

All in all, God is always smiling, from above
On converted Jews, and kids in love.

Taking a Leave

I knew I would cry and feel bad – feel
Sorry for you, dad. It is that nothing that we all
Share as we come into the world: men, women
All lovers of life – all lonely at times
Speaking of love in rhymes, of hate as if it were
The funny side of Fate…

We walked the same earth. We even slept
Together – you, holding my hand – Me, listening
To your heavy, prolonged breaths, feeling
Your firm grasp giving me peace in darkness
Giving you love in silence. Being there
For each other, being –

We shared the same house, which you left behind
Which left for me now seems so unfulfilled
And I feel empty too, without you
Walking through the distilled air, remembering
You – everywhere. How does it feel?
Memories can kill…

We lived for each other for a while, sharing
The rosebushes you planted, the orange tree
That owes you life – like me. You grew into it all
The smells and scents and sensations
Peregrinations of our feline beasts, small
Mysteries of life you planted –

It is all here, grown with your giant hands
Your smile, your large, forgiving eye.
Good people should not die, I whisper
As I pen these lines, after weeping, calling out
No reply, safe for the ethereal existential angst
A strange linguistic quandary…

I am a Hamlet on the rise, I speak to dark places,
In becoming Good myself. I feel free, I fly
Goodness rests in me. Maybe you just had too much
And gave some of it to me... Maybe, you knew that I
Would be left behind with a story to tell
Genius under a spell I sing –

Spirits inhabit the smallest thing. Perhaps, I
Make them up, because I cannot cope with death.
It is too much to take, so I pretend
There is a foreign land on the horizon and we
Are bound to meet again one day – I believe I am
The greatest of pretenders then…

I hope you had a very pleasant trip, some company
A voluptuous maiden could keep up with you
For a while, at least. I too pretend
You missed my mum, who had had to depart
Long time ago, and waited on the shore, waiving
Waiving with her Heart –

Sometimes, it is much easier to pretend
As my Man said, to think that you are close
There in the mountains in a pretty house,
Reading James, playing a fiddle, watching T.V. –
Forget Common Sense! It is too common here
Things remain – men disappear…

Why should things that we do not need exist? Why
People without Love or Faith should live? Why
Do I have to be a stoic, solipsist, Empedocles kind? Why
Left behind to wander on? They say that
Women can bear it... Makes me mad. I recall Socrates
I smile now, thinking this —

We all have what it takes, be it Will or Reason
House for a rainy season, equipped with Eternity
Each of us a tiny God, making the other one divine
Merely by trying to keep the promises we gave
Because our deeds are parts of our dreams
Large as the Human Heart...

We slave. We struggle on. We start anew each day.
We say prayers and graces and do Good.
We are the human race, trying to understand
Misunderstood, we seek each other constantly
Upon the stars, in the mountains, in the sea
We wonder why, we wander on —

May I kiss you on the cheek again? May I
Take leave of you now? Thank you for the smile.
The Earth is such a lonely place...
Let us be happy for a while —

In Search of a Fallen Star

Let us go now – cross that field
Once again to sunset rise
A Passing that a tear will yield
Passing the wheat-field Paradise

Let us enter one more time
The Past that we did sow together
Unabashed, in pantomime
Grasp and hold what has been severed

Let us sing a song of lovers
That knew each other long ago
Now as distant sisters, brothers
Striven in timeless, endless flow

Recall with pain our sunset strolls
Nature's whim, a late-bird's twitter
Naked night – our wishes, goals
The feelings that have grown so bitter

Why! Laugh, laugh at us, on a lurch
In search of a fallen star…
So fast time has passed – so slow
Are memories to leave the Heart

To leave us empty, filled with longing
To leave us lonesome, far apart.

Dream-shells

Sea-shells thrown out by the sea
Unheard and unseen now
Night slowly falls on you and me
Far apart, we cannot bow
          We cannot be

Some two thoughts on the shore
Muted and mellowed by the tide
Crystal-clad – and then – no more
Somehow, something is not quite right
          Quite as should be

Us, waiting for the stars to rise
The skies to grow less shallow
Metaphysics of endless trials
Not satiated yet, not sallow
          Not Enough Are We

A shadow game of chess we play
The King and the Queen – a pose?
Coming and going tide of day
Not like the twitch of your nose,
          And unlike Me

A mermaid dreaming of her Prince
Counting the sheep as minutes pass
Breaking the count with a wince
Watching them, a herding mass
          A Mystery

The stars, the sheep – all black-and-white
Without an ending is this night.

Church of Love

I have seen the story played over and over again
Jane Austen in a new-fangled gown – just as vain
A self-righteous beast waiting on the shore
To be picked up and carried across, as many did before
As this one does, and many after her will too
Poor ferrymen – they do not have a clue!

The watch the shore and the river is their trade
They hearken to the superficial bubble made
By the roughly buried oar into the laughing wave
Each is proud of his bark, a master, not a slave
Running errands or toiling with a chore at all
They are the giants of this Eden after Fall

It is a shallow paradise, for shallow people
For you and I, the river runs much deeper
Then there is a bent, a bolder with a twist
Before the waterfall, a wall of mist
And down below, after the roar and spew
Emerges the ever peaceful Me and You

It should be strange that we should fall to rise
It should seem unlike what they would call is *nice*
Somewhat out-of-order in an extraordinary way
Somewhat unlike you-and-I, they say
But then, they turn to the pier and, looking back
They smile and say: There's nothing that we lack

But it has been too long, and we rest far away
From that river now that we sailed yesterday
By the ocean in the garden of our dreams
Everything is far away, everything but seems
It is the seams of the seeming people
That gives our island the holy grail, a steeple

The Church of Love, filled with Blessing, unawares
For there is no-one of the *seeming* ones that cares.

My Fingers

My fingers are birds in flight
Hungry, inconspicuous, and wild
Hardly innocent – in the light of day
Hardly the fingers of a child

Gratefully plodding away
Raking words from the meadows of my Mind
Ending my arms in a stringent sway
Hardly anything but kind

I watch them as they weave
The paler mirror of my Dream
Out of my Heart to wreathe
Their own unearthly scheme

Learnēd and lazy they smile back
Waylaid but never lost
Without them – what would I be?
Would I lack substance – be a ghost?

They rotate around me
They pour Me down – my very Soul
I follow graciously
Ravenous birds out of control.

Deep at the Bottom of that Sea

Mendacity! again… Jealousy!
Vainer the sea of jealousy –
Few unvanquished ships of love
And the Moon far above –
Modestly at her staff she sits
Quietly meets the greenest wit
To shut her with a cloud of dust –

To shut him with a star or two
Across the poles of galaxies
Upon the seas of love –
But to the bottom none can see
There nothing lives, and probably
One day they too will bury me
Deep at the bottom of that Sea.

This Life You Know

A few walks in the park
A "Hello" – "Good-Bye" before sleep
Hours dance to Stravinski's bark
Some concerto – one pill deep

A shopping in two – a child one day
A simple, rather common Wish
Lovely dinner – a bedroom play
Savoir vivre – make it *riche*!...

There is a Law to Life – and I
Am a Traitor, still at large
Running to stall – to cast the die
Die unseen, without *equipage*

Five fingers fall apart
Faculties falter – flail and fall
Wild is the Will to strive
Will's the wildest call…!

Thus is the human Heart:
Hello? – Who? What? Where?
This brief and precious thing called Life
Nothing! Safe for the Will to Care.

Bury Me Where the Roses Pine

Bury me where the roses pine
Along the walls and verdure here
In this garden that we shared
That was our joy and faith and fear

Bury me – to make me Thine
Forever share me with this land
Land this wish and place this dime
Upon the tombstone with no name

A lucky coin for some merry time
Time married to the roses wild
For a coin – a lonely columbine
Gone with the wind, a playful child

Bury me to the bamboo chime
Below the sky, the Milky Way
Way-lay with memory that rhyme
Of Might or Would or Could or May

Bury me in this gleeful clime
And turn the page and start again
And have a smoke, and sip of wine
And be merry, forget the pain!

Bury me where the roses pine
Along the walls and verdure Dear
Lay me still – distil my crime
The crime of Love, the crime of Fear

That in this garden that we share
Took root, and ought to disappear.

Song of Graces

Gracefully among roses and full moon
Pining for Truth under the Milky Way
Sobering up from midnight gloom
I whispered *Good-Bye* to Yesterday

Thoughtfully – out of time and tune
With the flight of solid spaces
Will you join me? Please, come soon
To taste true love in well-known places

Among rose-buds and full moon
Or some sun-filled afternoon in Spring
Past memories, past midnight gloom
A chalice of Passion let us raise and drink

Of honeydew and morrows new
May the birds forever sing!

Sheep of Days

Days go by – meekly, without a wink
Sheep under the Gate of Time
And return once, perchance, upon a rhyme
Out of compassion spoken

Once striven by the fates they sink
Into the blithe oblivion of Time
As if to remember were a crime
And some sacred wow were broken

They have shunned the beasts of the woods
May have grasped the Mandrake by the roots
Have they smiled with the Sun touching the ocean?
Have they tasted the bittersweet potion of Life?

But they come-and-go, as they should
As if they had a notion, as if they understood –
Sheep without emotions – days without Strife
Bees blindly coming and going to their hive

Thus, meekly, without a wing they fly
Before we say: "Good morning" – and – "Good night"
They whisper their "Good-Bye"
And vanish out of sight.

Dancing Drops of Rain

Raindrops dance in strangest poses
Pink clouds dressed in bows of rain
Throw their magic on lonely roses
Victims with a human name

It is the wind that spells that name
The birds that chirp it in your ear
Nothing stays the same again
When the Time of Love is here

Someone should come and say:
Administer in small doses,
Wait till the symptoms quite appear

Wait till the perpetrator goes away
Or the deeper Self disposes
Of pleasure, sin, and fear –

Wait till the sky is clear… but *Nay!*
Each raindrop bears that name
Leaving a stain behind

On the window-pane of my Mind
On the inroads of my Heart.

Oh, Love, Carry Me forth!

Oh, Love, carry me forth, onwards, up
Up to the Sky where I can rest with Thee
Be kind, be blind, be as Thou art
Plumed for this brave start
And fair to whom in truth Thy findest

Past loneliness, and vacant spaces, up
Through the constellations ever kindest
Across poles, and hemispheres,
Where all apprehensions disappear, there
Point bravely beyond earthly pains and fears

Oh, Love, carry me closer to the Sun
I scream, I writhe, I refuse to believe in Fate
Who has not the Face, the Heart, the Hand
Which can reach and pray and understand
Thou hast shown me from the start

Touch me! Feel me! Please, return too soon
Lest too late Thou findest dust,
No tale left, and no-one left to tell
Of the spell, the enchantment, the mystery
That may have never ended, safe for Thee

For this Universe that Thou wieldest now
Thou hast the power to likewise un-fate, disavow.

Calyx of Wishes

There was a spell of golden flowers
No field – no magic, seemingly
Marigolds? – some tiny suns
Heaving their heads dreamingly

It was in early afternoon
In an untimely falling year
Side by the Sun and the Moon
That my inattention places here

Negligible – numberless – no fear
Each craving that one Moon
The Sun of suns that resting here
Draws a sigh and sings in tune

In wonder that we wandered on
Strolled down to the ocean
Was it a river? Raft? One image gone
Daffodils would have no notion

Their petals in motion – waiving hands
To the breezes of our Paradise
A calyx of wishes – a Dream that blends
And plays with me now as I rise.

Forgetting to Remember

Life is a journey from here to there
And to remember makes it sweet
Love and someone for to care
The Mystery runs beat by beat

Resolving goals and getting ready
Revolving round the eclipsed Heart
Reflecting – lever-like and steady
Man is much too much too smart…

He must be leaving unaware
Must believe yet never know
The gown this hummingbird shall wear
The stars in me that night has sewn

This raindrop fall he will not see
The moonlight silver on this cloud
No, tonight is deemed to be
Lonely, lingering all about

Then, with a prolonged sigh he'll say:
The puzzles I have solved…
A flicker of an eye – children's play
Thus the Earth has revolved…

Then he will give away a sacred nod
And change the channel too
Somewhere far away is God
Watching over me and you

As we fall asleep by the TV screen
Forgetting to remember where we've been.

A Land to Share

There is an entire Land out there
A whole new, vast continent
Does it scare or thrill you? Do you care?
For you and me this Land was meant

No deserts there, mountains are rare
Horizon-painted, canvass-deep –
No, this Land is not barren, is not bare
There, we will never wake to only sleep!

Who knows it, is free to share
To learn the role, and take the part
My crimson Soul, my golden hair
Green in the eye, the bluest Heart…

There is an entire Land out there
It scares and thrills me, because I care
That Land is Me – that Land is You
The most beautiful, and true.

Familial

My mother was a mad cow
My father was killed by the Reds
My sister died in a strange row
Blacklisted by the KGB, the local Feds
I struggled, and I made it, but now
Thinking of it makes me mad
I made it – ask me not how
The story would be much too sad...

You would see a rabbit strung
By the tail and skinned
While the International was sung
Blood dripped from me, and thinned
I became a chimera, a vulture true
Out of necessity did I sin
And I would hate telling you
Quite exactly what I mean...

Let us just say, I had my share of Hell
And fitted myself for any season
Now, I am perhaps free to tell
But there is no sense in it, no reason
What is Hell anyway but a strange spell
In a foreign land of foreign people
Who want to shuck and shell you
Strike your Soul, strike deeper...

So, my mad cow memories disperse
As I imagine what I recall
Now as a phrase, a line, a verse
A fleeting phantom, some unanswered call…
Rabbits like me are somewhat sparse
No-one will make us to a thrall
A slash! A slash! – a scar in the Heart?
The Heart, they never touched at all!

Bound to Each Other

The tics that bind us to each other
Two stars – two mysteries – two lovers
Inalienable, ineluctable, undercover
Like spies or – rather – thieves
We steal the leaves that gather
At the feet of God.

He, with a smile, lets us play
With the stars along the Milky Way
So that, perhaps, down below
The others will look up, and learn
And know that the stars above
Speak of Love.

The Sun and the eternal skies
Eternity floating upon a kiss
A tale sung of in lullabies
Something you must have, or miss –
The Bond, not of will or right,
Not ours – but His.

That Will never dies
That Right, that Truth, that Kiss.

Upon the Common Land

Sometimes dying is so close that I can hear it breathe
Invidious and inviting – breathing to deceive
Sometimes she is at my shoulder and I smile
We have walked another mile and closer stand
Somewhere half-way – upon the common land
"I cut no compromises," she would say to me
"As always," I should smile but never flee
Stare ahead and all around – as if in a dream
Unable to help it – unable to scream, forsaken
Taken by her whim, twisted, shaken
Broken down and proven worthless worm
Taken by the heel and wrist and bathed
In Lethe's stream – shorn of memories and more
Humble once again – to the marrow, to the core
Sometimes, dying is so close that I can see her
One arm sneaking from behind the CD rack
The other pressing the mattress beside my head
They sound a cacophony of spooky sounds
In between the tick-tock on the wall she abounds
I take my will and pull the clocking wall apart
2am – the countdown of my heart begins
Over again. I am not dying at anybody's whims
Though it might seem that I am.

Stating My Case

I state my case now, for it'd better be
Stated correctly, put down to history,
For history is something that we make
Minute by minute, day by day –

So here I stand and will not pray
For you to read my cause as I dispatch
As I propose it to you, as a match
Of minds that know what they desire

That they dream, though little that they require
Like I – arisen from the Old World ashes
Transported with no grave crashes
To the stars and stripes, and rays of light

Now – moonlit night – a yawning porch
Light in the lurch but all the same
Inside of Me – not just a word – a name
Some ultimate blurt, a *may* of *must*

Living not for an accolade, a bust
Next to your Pallas, pinhead podium
For amnesiac academia – what odium!
But for a simple pleasure of the play –

May history be what it may.
What is more than you and I together?
What is more than today for you and I?
Tell me – or should I?

Nothing. Tonight I will sleep like a cat
Curled, my feet up in the air, my head
Twisted and twined, my chin up, awaiting destiny
What academia can better me?

Upon the Sun Today

Is it not strange – when the morrow comes
The sun sneaks in and under
Where we pitched our restful sleep
The day rises to do its duty, to keep Time alive
Something we could not ever do
But for that wake-up call to me and you…

Is it not strange – two strangers to bide the call
The serendipity of Spring and Fall
Of any season, of any motion
How vain – to entwine us in this commotion!
And then to make us stand by a rose, a tree
Enclosed by four walls again – you, and me
Made to feel great in feeling small
Inept, ungainly, rolling the Ball of Time
Afloat with senses on a senseless rhyme…

Is it not strange – when we come together
That we should want to part?
Go back to the unseen land, the country of the Heart
Where the remotest outpost, without light
The darkest corner of the darkest night
Makes us warmer than the high noon of today
Makes us feel at home while far away in Time…

How strange, how sad the dawn for you, for me
If we cannot see each other – if we cannot see
Today as more than a silly rhyme with "yesterday"
And tomorrow but as a vague call by Him
Who knows it all, that of His whim
We rise, we fall, we meet – take leave…
Take leave? Does seeing mean to disbelieve?

The Old Fountain

The old fountain, broken, falls apart
In the corner of the Heart
He penetrates the matter to the root
The stone covered in smoggy soot
Remains. Water will beat the matter
Tides come and go. What is better
Falling rain that drop-by-drop erodes it
Evaporating images – wholly fit
To disappear in the seamless past
Or to nail it on the mast?
To kill the nightmare with a precision blow
He would do it, but does not know how
Without prejudice, predestined to succeed
To evolution fit, dropping on the stone – he
All alone.

The Beasts in My Brain

I splinter in the setting Sun
I run with my nylon stocking – run
To become Eternity

At the bottom of my foot, somewhere
I stare into distance – I hesitate, in fits:
Shall I believe in Fate?

Playing cards and counting days
Always have one more
And one more… and then?

The stars that splinter in the Sun
The water dropping on the edge
The dirt upon the window ledge –

Tiny, invisible, I am
A stain upon the window-pane
Eaten by your Eye

The Beasts in my brain
Am I – ?

To Hell and Back

I have been in hell –
It might have been heaven too
But since you were not there
It was hell

All animals, all together
Waited for some pot of luck
Staring at me – was I it?
Not a wink

Yet, it was a dream, I think
Because it was so true
And left me not a clue
As to the spell

So, it must have been hell
Because the blood boiled on the slabs
Of marble mummy heads
In zero gravity –

Then I woke up, slowly spelling
Your sweet name – alone again

Nothing... you know
Nothing is the same.

Dreaming On

Flamingos somewhere down in Africa
Hunted by Baboons and caught
Escaping yet – never quite "Ah-ah-ah!"
Mating out of sight
A crock's lifeline – spider's "Shah!"
Fishing for life just spawned
Self-substantial to the bone
Over and on and in between
Sharks upon the T.V. screen…

I fall asleep in dreams of death
In distant drone a-drape
I drown, at the bottom take a breath
Time is the master
Evolution is a slave

The dawn returns in a swoon
I rise, still dreaming – dreaming on
Part Flamingo – part Baboon
At least the sharks are gone.

Uncle Phil

I have my books – what else do I need? – uncle Phil said
Smiling, whiling away the day – somewhat mad at me
Somewhat for the others – to see that they
Have really very little – or nothing at all
Expire unrecognized, unawares – perishing small
A cog in the wheel and a history turned bad
Eggs that had frozen in time once before – to become
Somewhat somehow something more in southern sun
By the Pacific shore wherein it all must happen
Yet – he had perished from Earth in the East
Swallowed by the curlew call and New World mist
Before you and I were up to it – unborn yet
Unfit altogether to see him seeing red
Crimson and grow pale over a book he had never read
Over a house he had never owned and never shall
For now he is gone – biting the dust – dead
No more fighting – no more mad
And what he knew or read
Nobody can tell…

Hairy Joe Schmoe

I met Joe Schmoe in the pool
He was hairy – furry – full of air and
The end of the world in the corner of the eye
He hurled himself with force at me
He was no fool… no small beer either
So he said, by-and-by

And kept smiling through the frothy edge
Of his mouth, mouthing somewhat
Of a wedge, barely cutting through
I am a knight, and
How are you? he said –

Joe Schmoe, all right
A lying, bad egg – a dime a dozen today
I drew a sigh: I'll be OK
Stop with that nag

I know a man who is true
Who will not play like you
At fishes and porcupines

He maybe away now
But left his Heart behind

I'll be OK, I said, if you don't mind –

I left the hairy Joe floating on hot air
God knows where…

Swept by Seasons

Another Fall – another Winter
As if the dead were calling from Beyond
You love this Land and yet
It is too distant and too sad at times
It is the Land of rugged rhymes and reasons
That rhyme with revival and setting Rights
With seasons always too much here
Yet out of sight and scope of understanding

Next snow upon the mountain peaks
Proximate cloud upon the sun
Subsequent victim – the one that seeks Beyond
Turns her head – procrastinating
Long before it had been said that she went mad
She knew that you were waiting
Always round the corner
Always in the season that swept by…

She did cry but nobody could see –
Do you believe in Destiny?

To All Those Who Speak of Old Masters

To all those who speak of old masters
Alabaster chambers and labors of the earth
Who mirth and exult in disastrous ends
That they bear forth new commencements

To all those who were while we were not
Believed in gold and god and genocide
Who would hide behind a marble column too
And whisper about me and you

To all those who drowned in the bowl
With goldfish on the prowl and persevered
Until the worse they feared arrived and
They called it Beginning – not the end

To all those who counted the seven ages
Divided life in stages and the stage perceived
With the poet and the sage who
Kept asking: Why stay so deceived?

To all those who loved their caves
Taught about slaves in schools, the old Rome
A gnarled gnome in every corner
Carefully guarding cold canvasses

To all those before me I now raise
This chalice, and in admiration do concede
That I do not pray for recognition
That I am but a naked flirt wholly fit
To be perused and thrown away
To sink to oblivion, the specters of history
With obsequious men, singing to the Old
Master, the Old Age, the golden days
Do not concern or disturb me.

Too many ancient wits make my head spin
I live to be – not to have been.

Learning Words

Judge – Jury – Executioner...
Just brushing on words for
Language that cannot fail you Sir
Sounds that sail upon high seas
Missing the port – safe haven
Very few safe but the truth
It remains as follows:
One borrows words from abroad
To make room for what sought
We never found – until
One day upon a marble slab
In letters that no-one recognizes
In a language long forgotten
The dead shall spell:
Words were siblings in a paradise
Un-begotten merchandise of foreign lands
Was it wise to learn
What no-one understands?

Dislikes of Like

years run like rabbits
and she swims upon them like a swan
and everything is like something else
oceans run like streams of tears
faces mouthing eyes that are like oysters in a soup
oysters that would like to dream
dreams of whipped cream – stars and galaxies
allegories of peregrinating actors
people that are always like something else
and while the tide locks the ship
thoughts wonder into foreign lands like birds
migrating over the mainland to the horizon of likenesses
because the end comes about like it should
so much like so many other things
in summersaults astern in the recoil of undercurrents in your wake
and the clouds pass by like oversized Mesozoic reptiles
while sailors feast on lobsters and prawns of the Permian age
never linking the likenesses of magnitudes
until one day just before dawn
one takes notice of a swan that looks like her –
just as stately and distant like
some last lonely star that the sunshine sweeps away...

Taking a Peek

Still here? I softly sweep the world away
I do not pray because
The eye within might sin again
Might take a peek through this unmended wall
A quick-headed peek, and behold!
There is a hungry look out there!
The world looking back at me...
The World where I want to be?

Cracked angles crumble and bend –
I see the outside, but fail to understand
I can hear singing from behind the corner
Hello! Is someone out there for me?
We must be here for each other, I strive to say...
Who will glance back at me awhile?
Who will be so kind as to help me stop the world?

Otherwise, I will have to mend this wall
That is all.

blue

softly sweeping through wasted days
she sways from the salons on Sixth Avenue
she says she is blue
through and through she says
and the other She – ? – listening silently
she used to be a Daisy once
she used to be so pure so unused so un-
depleted she steps up and lights a cigarette
her days are wasted – wasted days
the television plays another comedy
she raises and goes to the bathroom sink
another drink?
another round of laughter from the distant room
faces that nobody can see
pre-recorded in their bloom
the mirror cries – the toothbrush swings
two eyes – two rings beneath them
days are faces are men smiling back
oh! – how they cannot laugh!
...and life is such a gag!

Verdammt!

I want to swear: *Verdammt!*
If I had known then what I know now
I would not have laughed
Neither under the Niagara Falls
(Oscar's wildest of "experience")
Nor downstream and off the boat
With Huck's "been there before"
Nor that frozen night before the war
When the Raven cawed "Never-nevermore"
And something died in us...
That is the problem – I should think
Some drink to bear it – others sink
It is the obverse side of the Sun
One can neither stare it in the eye nor run
Lest one should die
But then – one would not be one but many
Which is very different
Verdammt!

Changing

The arena cheers – desperate for a kill
I carry that image with me still
Everywhere I go – from Toledo back
To Vienna-Salzburg-Halls
To London, the theatre-land,
Overpopulated Paris, small and bland,
Prague, *piqué* with pantomime and concertó grosso
Then I wonder through unsightly caves and veer away
Brussels is buried in rain and Marseille
Rains human souls for a change – *parlez-vu quoi?*
All of the arena dwellers gone, I am here
I carry on to the old Crete, for Minos to meet
And then – the Greeks are everywhere!
An olive on my martini, please
And all eyes are upon me as I awake –
You see what is at stake is life
The Roman Fever is still around, Isabelle
And I have many a story to tell
While for the better part of my heart, I pray to be
Free from the boulders of the past
And it has a worse part too – like yours
And loves changing the course with rhymes
And cheers the old times.

Waiting for the Stars to Pass

Here I remain – patient me
But my eyes closed
Waiting for the stars to pass
For the day to reappear
As soothsayer and seer the Moon
Smiles back at me…

So she has done through history
So we have always done
Ever since Time began his rounds
Ever since the first black hole
The first supernova sounds and
The sins of Eve began…

Other souls passed above too
Upon the skies that cherished them
As they now carry me to you
In a delightful lullaby
To the land far above, where
Not even the eagle dares arise

I adorn my thoughts with distant suns
The paradise of moons and stars
Through tonight into tomorrow
I run through centuries
Through lives and sorrows of the past
To the future that is here to last

I run and yet remain, as my Love – parting forever
Forever here to stay.

Closing Eyes

It takes more than one sense
To drown and resurrect a specter
To see beyond the shadows
That spread over shorter days
"Someone prays" – Caesar said
And I would be moved too
Thinking that prayers would do it
Win over time and space
How come you are around
When you are no more?
How come love remains to disturb
The Galaxy – the Universe – the Orb?
I take the cup you drank from too
And fill it with hot tea
Still – it smells like weeping willows
And it tastes like memory
I close my eyes – there is
Nobody my eyes could see – .

One Very Pretty Day

Her eyes discoursed of cloudless sky
Of something that I knew too well
Without a syllable, a word did I
Join in the echo of her spell

Worlds apart we grew, over the years
Eons, rather, of humanesque endeavor
A wisp of wind, a-weep without tears
Resemblances age could not discover

On a lonely bench in the autumn park
That year, as good as any other
That year to meet, to tell, on a lark
Is it not funny what we discover?

I thought aloud, but she would not say
Abstracted, aloof, her eyes a-wonder
A player on a podium, a show, a play
Orchestra in the pit beneath…

My heart has not drunk or eaten
For many months, years perhaps
My feet feel feeble, my knees weakened
I spoke slowly, words would lapse

Never mind… suddenly, she awoke
Rising up from a long, longing swoon
Glanced ahead, and softly spoke
I wish you a lovely afternoon!

After she left, I mused and slowly rose
Grasped firmly on my walking stick
I put the picture back in my purse
Flattered myself, and felt so *chic*

Never mind... with abandon, I did say
For it was a very pretty day indeed
And whether you stand and walk, or sit
Life is more than just a skit

An old picture for discourse, an old friend
A memory that is hard to comprehend.

Where Are You?

While you roam in those caverns
Measureless to men, I must remain
Washing off the stain of remembrance
Many remembrances and many stains
Somewhat haughty – almost vain
Counting and re-counting my miles
The miles I have taken in Time and Space
Musically filled with the harmony of spheres
Smiling at naiveté of Socrates and
Chasing Schrodinger's black cat
From the neighborhood, out of my head –
All in all – doing what I should
Lurking – luring – wondering and
Of Wonder never cured – serene
As a she-snake on a scorching stone
Perfectly sprawled, without a turn
Turned to the Sun, just feeling the air
Where memories are veering with the gulls
Little soft white waves get swept away
By larger once while the day turns
Into nights – cavernous and measureless again
Something in me yearns –
The sea – the sea – the sea deep inside Me
Is craving endlessly: Where are You?
Why are you not with Me…?

Meeting Death

The first time I encountered death it was
Invisible – then at home it assumed
Potato color of the past – tainted land
Sinfully beautiful and crude it died.

It was Death died upon me, and I went
To bury her outside
I was five and my father said we should
Bury her – the It of Her – the hue-less hare
With one leg broken and the other
Back in the permafrost of gust and dusk
One limpid eye laughing back: See! See!
I made it! Will you follow me?

I did not – so she returned in another form:
A kestrel of a sparrow on the window sill
Flew in and knocked his head upon the top
The luster of cut glass and a whitewashed wall
And he was gone – so small and so soon
A bandaged wing – no will to be, to survive
So we went out and stayed a mass
And lay him in the ground

The march hare slept near by that spot
My father gave me a hug and whispered in my ear:
It is all right – he is an angel now, and here
I wept and knew that like the hare
It was Death out there
I knew he would rot in the rigid soil
He would wait while we toil above
He would laugh at human love and fear
Always under our feet – too far to touch
And much too near to look aside
Unseemly oversight

Somehow or other – I encountered death before She
Really had a chance to tally Me
I would shake the cold, white fingers of her hand
I would spell her name and She would understand
I would look where she malingers in the ground
By a russet shag in the woods, where I
Once fed a most beautiful doe, spinning dreams
About how the world was just for me and her
(And a prince on a white horse, of course)
And where she did die, it seems…

Somehow or other – I went always out
Last time upon the tallest house it town
By the lightening rod – awaiting the chimney sweep
With a secret that I could not keep
That I could not keep any longer to myself, for
I knew better then, and could converse with Death
Like only witches can

By then, dying was the last thing that would matter
To me, and you have to be where I was to know
For it has always been, shall always be
Death resembles someone that we know –
She looked like my crazy mother at times
At times, She took my rhymes away from me
With my father and my home and the end
Leaving me behind, all alone, and weeping
Under the Matterhorn, by the Mediterranean sea,
Now by the Pacific willows, and the Jasmine tree,
The silent mimes of stars that nurture me again

The first time I encountered Death it was
With my father in a Silesian field
The last time She smirked back from my father's eye
Then someone just as close did die, and now I am
To meet the pertinacious monster once again
Coming in with a creak of the heavy wooden door
And walking by my bed on a squeaky floor
Why! She is like a fly that buzzes after dark
She has no manners but a lot of spark
So here I am to give her a piece of my mind
To teach her how to knock and be a little kind
Let me watch T.V., eat, and meditate
And Live! Everything else? – Call it Fate!

Creepy Feeling

I have this creepy feeling
                deep in my bones
                              she said
Last time I felt like this
                was when they came
                              with rain
Unseasonable people at
                an unseasonable time
                              but I
Had nothing then to give
                not a even worn-out rhyme
                              a memory
Look at me today –
                Say, can you see the feeling
                              in my bones?
It comes out of seasons
                like those people then
                              won't heal
Won't leave me alone
                won't and won't but
                              overkill the stay
For them life is a lie
                made up of what you can
                              and cannot touch
They come with rain
                and leave drought behind
                              for me, as for me
I hate this creepy feeling
                I just want to be
                              thank you very much.

Let's Go

Darling? Are you ready? Let's go!
We must be on time for the show...
So you stand up – to perform the last rite
You do not mean to do much but you do it anyway
You look in the mirror – a long stare
Something in it that you cannot suffer – cannot stay...
Silent walls? Messages? Pictures? An old photograph?
No! Nothing must distract you now...
Darling? Let's go! Let's go!
Is this you? Is this face and body You or –
Does it merely seem to be? Was it something else before?
Was it you as you are – or are you what you never were?
Was it something else? Perhaps something more?
Or something less? Because, deep within, I feel
This fear – this feeling low...
Darling? Let's go!
As you shed your skin and find another *you* within
All that you can see is your father's face, and
It scares you so... *Father?* Only you would know
There is no other knowing now – . Come,
Recite your *Gunga Din*, and *Captain, Oh!* – My Captain
So I fear – where shall we go from here?
Let's go! Let's
Escape that simple common fear, as common as the flu
The fear that our road is near the end
The fear that the other one is the real you
The fear that that one day you will rise and stand up
Pass me by and never remember, recollect
But for a picture on the wall...
Darling! Let's go! Let's go!
It's high time for the show!

All Hapless Human

I wake up in the middle of the night
I wake up to the night I wake
Up and somnambulate
Medea weeps and wails within
Revenge and sin and I
Dreaming, passing by
The wind laments on the roof
My head spins around the house,
Comes to, and
The end?

Maybe she will not kill this time
Maybe, if she wakes up
To a kiss sublime…
Like this – light as air
Flying to the stars
Falling with the stars
I am here, and there - everywhere
Am I?

All anguish all
A hapless human Heart…

The Penultimate Day

The penultimate day of the year:
Sauerbraten and sauerkraut and the end is here
And all is sour in my German mind except
You and the City of ravens and desperados

As if this City were not its people
As if this Sky was truly what it is –
A beautiful, boundless Universe
Spelling Love in a single verse…

Ich habe Verständnis of a squirrel
With a very long tail…
Deep within I weep and wail and lie to myself
Life goes on regardless –

Winter crept in and we still struggle
Watching lollipops – how lickerish am I!
Always aloft – forever in the Sky
My eye tinted green and blue and gray…

It is the penultimate day of the year
Time to celebrate. I draw a sigh, a line, right here:

Pray – tell me – how could you and I
Ever, ever die…?

Eternal Love

Eternal Love – she said
Sounds like a brand of cigarettes
Or a washing powder
A shampoo perhaps, like *Two-in-One*
Wet, fast-drying nothingness –
God bless and good-bye
All in all, a puffery, a lie
With a big smile and a kiss…

So, *what is there to miss?*

Perhaps something undead yet
That not even Scheherazade would know
Vampire-like, full of want and vesting
With some ancient virgin dream…

No olden days – nothing in between?
Nothing after. Before
Her and him, before
You and me – what remains?

From Tupperware parties and Tiffany rendezvous
From the strolls along neon-lighted avenues
From promises and corralled sheep
When two were one, and none could sleep?

Because it was *Eternal Love*
Down by the bridge, the Camelot, the seven seas…

So what is there to miss?

Mon-stir

Nostradamus dead and gone – who are we
to go like this – trying on
a new destiny?
dismissing his meditations –?
(falling asleep again…) then (that is: I)
waking up – as women or men or
the rest – still (on the mend?)
in an intricate dawn launched upon the canvass of a pre-surreal one –
mon-stir
lock and cock and barrel – one wilderness
stir of the tide under the ship – one ocean, one sea
diverging *mon a clef* – currents flowing into foreign lands
follow me – the unharvested heap of human heads
fallow me (brains come later)
racemes of our lives – with an attitude today, say
will you stay in your vibrant dive – nude
the birds and the bees taking off without you
taking a consensus on Happiness
then on park benches hidden away from tumult
from the sight of the other world
the butts and ends of the otherness
very truly yours – sincerely
ends without heads – life
piece-meal me: ah!
mon-stir
de *miel* turned sour (a misnomer too)
a bard too new to like or enjoy
calling love "some epidemic glue" or toy…
and my chivalric notion cont-
inuous – sin-inuous end – out of use
an eggshell scowling back at a cross, a dying swan
silence please – music for a queen begins

may I have this dance? – come, com-
motion – ex-pack-tation – the last chance: ah!
2112 *deluge* 30-something then another Tunguska
closer to the sun predicting death and new
beginningssss....
the in-deeans in why-oming still sing and roam
generations grow up to the predictions they do not know
and we fall asleep
asleepasleepasleep...
without a stir, *mon ami*

When the Dead Begin to Sing

When the dead begin to sing
To sing to you in rhyme
Thus-and-thus, the authorities say
Have a drink, have some wine
While they still hang around
Growing out of time with you
Growing under your skin
Passing into another di-mention
Somewhat more real and true
Than you ever knew they could be
Sipping of your morning tea
Feeding birds on the bench with you
Stroking your cat, ever so gently
You doggy wants some too...
Some of the world where no-one will
Intrude or ever really care
Passing lifetimes with a single stare
A fleeting sigh: anybody there?
It is the dead begin to sing
From dog-eared paperbacks
Plodding through your mind in dreams
Too inquisitive to please
Plotting their own schemes of creation
In dirges, in silly rhymes spelling
Pre-destination – foreordained
Illusion-clad and classified: for you
Top secret this one dead, new
Skeleton of *Geheimnis*
(which means "mystery" over there)
We were there too, they say
We were like you – believed in Life
Some things survive though

But no-one at all can see through
Distant cocoons, darker demises
Purgatorioes in throes of thrills
Some like it to be chained, as you know
Past dismay? Meet me, and then –
Meet another me between the lines that
Will not be dead!
Nonchalantly, I spell out a worn-out rhyme
In search of Happiness

The dead speak without asking
Then sing, and I sing along:
What is, is – what is this
Geheimnis of otherness?
Some German heart imbued with
The American Soul
A ghoul painted in green upon the bluest sky
Why? Who am I? Meeting the dead
And never dying
Painted in the sad-mad flaking pale...
Forcing myself to cry, crying
(Was that a smirk of concept in your eye?)
Yet, I cannot fail you –
Trust in Wodan and Thor and Me
It is good philosophy to cherish
The turtle, the elephant, the Human Eye
Omnia mea... never lie
About the dead, carry it all on your back
Like a turtle, a snail with his sack
Too small for a good neighbor
Too large for a real habitation
Every move a labor of life, peregrination
Too slow for the dead...
Is it not sad that none of them can run?
None will outlast the Universe?
But the end of the story, the end of this verse?
The dead have had their say tonight

Much too terse and much too out of sight
Only the echo remains
To stain your Heart like a child stains the sheets
(A twitch in your eye? You do not want to die?)
The silence after is the Truth
Even if the word before
Was such a silly lie…

All We Are

Was it a snowflake? Was it a star?
I could not tell for it was so far
Was it a He or was it a She?
For all that Beauty I could not see

I could not grasp an atom of sense
I could not move – was all in suspense
Suspended Time – afloat in Space
Only a rhyme for His Divine Grace

Was it a year before the fall?
Ten thousand? One, and one more?
Was it just now, a minute ago
A heartbeat of silence – the heartbeat I know...

Eons have passed, and we wonder on
Eternal Fall – Spring, and anon!
Perceive but Beauty all through and through
As I did, and do – as He does you

A snowflake or a falling star –
One Wish is all We are.

A Memory to Beseech

The Sun passes into distant snows
Memory retires – the night cushions us in
We recall what the North star knows
And thus whisper from our sleep
Wherein spirits, ghosts unseen – creep
Intangible ghosts of not-so-long-ago
Come to sing softly by our side
Borne of where they were used to go
One breath upon another, heaping
A multitude of mysteries:
Rays of sunshine, flakes of snow
Reverberating echoes of the deep
Drown, dissolve us in eternal peace…
In the sounds of clashing images
Smells and colors that we want to seize
Upon the expiring lip, in the quiet room
The essences appearing like the frieze
On the poet's ancient urn, to bloom
To blossom in us, to forever please
With memories of some long-forgotten afternoon
Of a day that may have been… and yet:

It is that sleep that drives us mad
It is that womb of eternal time we know
That wonder of the touch of yesterday
That shows us not where to go, but
Rather, makes us long for where we have been
And makes us mad for we cannot win over Time
But for a reverie, an ephemeral rhyme
Which too will disappear with the morrow light… and yet:

Would we want an eternal night? To be
Ruled by an image, a figment of memory? To be
Frozen in a step, singing with the sea? To be
Suspended in between the Sun and the Moon
On the hot air of our expired desires
Past wishes, slumbering fires, embers of the mind
Cushioned in under the reflection of our Star
Until we awake again, to find it too far...

Invisible, and beyond reach, another's find
Another's memory to beseech...

In Throes of Fleeting Shades

Sideswept the moon shoots her smiles
And we smile back unwittingly
May last this ephemeral while
Under the shadow – fleeting shade
Relish the moment soon to fade
Find succor in the stars above
Let us seek where the comets play
The tales of time and timeless love
Fear no specter of the ancient Man!
Sense but the eruptions of the Sun!
Our faculties make little ken
Know not – and will not run!
We will not run with the night sidewept
We shall not perish by the moon
We will not weep where others wept
And shall not dye in a dying swoon –
Tonight shall last a thousand
                    and a day
A song we sung shall never pass
                    nor fade away.

I Speak to You

I speak to you, my dreams, my Dream
In the midnight air against the sky
Invisible spots upon an unseen butterfly –
Am I or am I yet to be?
Am I a part of you or are You a part of me?
To lie below – be lie that lying not to know
That maggot-mirth may maim the Heart
Mesmerized midst the mid-day flair
For you, my dreams, I fly and flare
I fall and fail – and – one more start…
How superstitious – how studious the Soul!
Pursue the pith – follow your goal!
What hides above the darkened sky?
Emerald and amethyst fight in the eye
A tear that unseen will nor dry –
A butterfly of many dreams
Painted on the wing am I – in between
The night above – and you, My Love.

Where else should love emanate
but from a peaceful heart?
Compassion absolved of jealousy or hate
Love from the very start –

Loving hearts harbor more
Than zeal for each other's Soul
Dreams divulge the ancient lore –
To protect is not Love's goal

Some proffer friendship in Love's stead
Some offer a smile and a lonely bed…
My bed is occupied with dreams
Of You, my Love, who sometimes seem

To come and go – a mirage on the midnight sky
Thus, with my dreams, I rise – I fall – I lie…

In Sorrows and Throes

All the birds are singing
                    and the sky is clear
And the Sun is on his way
                    and the stars are near
Always lying by – always
                    so am I:

The Eye that wonders high above
The Heart that seeks her only Love
The Ear that tarries for a sound
Of the footsteps on the ground –
Just the Bluebird eyes me sharp
How come this lady hath no harp?
Did Orpheus or Zephyr seize it
Disappearing in the breeze?
Tell me birdies – tell me trees
In your wise and tow'ring Crown
Where the Sun's ray always reaches
Is my Beloved – is he there?

Or is he eating other peaches
                    by the distant shore
Sailing on, sailing more, more
                    leaving me but hopes?
Leaving me to my longing
in sorrows and throes?

A doggie tongue licks my face
Fluffy the Cat throws circumspect glances
The Bluebird even makes advances from the tree
Pomegranate sunshine reaches me –
And the stars can see and feel my grace
Flow with grief and sorrow in the face
The Moon, the great-grandmother to us all
Gives me a wink and sooths my call
The call into the night that she understands
Full of pale desire that never ever ends
A thousand twitters more and a sigh
On a bough rests the sad and lonely I
I lonely and sad rest by that bough
Hoping that you can hear me now:

For the Moon – she knows
                              the stars can see
How much – how much…
                              how much I long for Thee.

An Echo of a Call

Darkness has settled all around
But I cannot sleep, cannot keep up with the sound
The sound of silent walls and draperies
The echo of spaces and of times
While others sleep I look around
Surprised at what my eyes have found –
A photograph upon the mantelpiece
A painting of sunshine a-float in the breeze
Caucuses of quietude on the ground
My feet but softly follow, promise-bound
The weight of tiles – a thousand memories
Emerald darkness, each step a goodnight kiss
No life – safe to appall or to astound
No breath, and yet the heart begins to pound
What is this? – Reason poses quandaries
Is this the path of "haves" or "might-have-beens"?
For I may have been a speck of paint upon the wall
And all this but an echo of a wishful call
A call that dreamt-up echoes in my head
A call from my Love that keeps me waiting – mad.

I Wonder

They sore suddenly – they hover high above
Tossing about in molecules of light
Parallel worlds – all a-leap for love
Keep me still, wakeful through the night

As birds of prey they soar to the Moon
Cadaver-lovers – eager to fight
Monsters of silent lore – no tune
No a chirp – no consolation for my plight

It is a sour and solemn performance
It is a poor and lonesome flight
It is eternity from here, from hence
To speak of love as some delight

To tell the tale of falling, falling deep
Of dreaming of the other world
In a daylight reverie – or in full sleep
To what adversity is one hurled!

And the other world, the other Me?
Does he wonder too? – or
Deep asleep, does he wander on –
                          wander peacefully?

Stringless You

People like to play You
The instrument – a stringless piece of solid sound
Bound by the ages of Springs and seasons of draught
Too loud to drown in
Too filled with itself, the world, the amplified beat
Speaks inside even while you are asleep
And then? Again –
Though somewhere deeper still
Wet, breaking sweat, worried without a will
Unholy ground of the primeval Nothingness
Things that but seem while the others
Intertwined and fearful – lovers afraid to lose
Compasses of dissolution…
Off to bed and muse for I
Gave Thee life – so let them not
Play You – the stingless, fearful – fretful You
Too tough not to be
Too soft to be true – .
I would not – cannot choose
But follow the sound the others make
Is there some mistake?
Is there anything else but echoless past
And future full of each-other?
I would rather not speak any more
I had better abstain
People play games and call it "war"
People play instruments and call it "love"
While your limbs grow sore
Several eons from now
I will be a holy cow again
Then I shall turn in awe
And return to you – .

Another Day

Another day – another night
Another ray of sunshine passes by
And out of sight…
So do You – so do I
For what we are, we are –
By virtue of the Sun
As the stars spell out the Future
As the Moon speaks of the past
But as to the Sun? Again, look up and see –
The sun is what we are:
Now or never, something says
Burning bright once more
And should we burn to death
By the breathless sunshine rays
Each with each as it plays
Another day – another night…
It shall be sweet to die:
We will embrace the dulcet Death
Because we knew Life sweet before
Because we knew Life sweet before
Before sweet Life we knew
After, we will know no more…

Falling in Love

I am the wonder of the raindrops
As I feel nothing, as I fall
Senses blunted by the dark
Whispers, wishes, warnings
Dreams that do not come till morning
Sounds like a running drop of rain
Again: yearning to feel, and to feel
No more…
Absence of all, where nothing
Where no-one – survives
Where desolation thrives:
Am I so vain or so desperate
To feel nothing when the world
Gone mad – screaming for more
Rains under my feet, upside-down –
Am I the one disowned by thee?
Am I the one to disown?
Turn me over in a rhyme
Just one more time, for the show
Let each drop of rain, let it be
A ray of Sunshine from you to me
A Valentine wish with a certain addressee…
For, undelivered, and in search we wonder
And keep falling, endlessly
As a raindrop falls for awaiting flower
Awaiting both –
Too long have we waited
Too weighty are our thoughts
With too much weight we fall –
Oh, what a weighty fall!

Silences

Cadaverous silences creeping around
Gatherings of ghosts – no sound
Safe wailing wind and weeping rain
Behind the door – so much pain
Leaving outside what comes not in
Living to leave it all – to win
Over temptations to stay and see
Becoming in being not as free
As the ghosts on the window-pane
As the midnight memories – the rain
That comes and goes in bouts
Like a fighter full of shouts
Raging in echoes of the silences
That twist and turn in cadences
That long-gone, still remain
In the beams of your house
In the marrow of your Heart...

Who Knows to See

When the time comes to search for roots
Like an old tree that cannot see too well
But teeters on the threshold of the dawn
With worn-out boots and peppery taste in the mouth
When the time comes... he says – but
Nobody is there to hear – himself
Searching, as he was his whole life through
Seeking to find the obtuse pith of being
Seeing nothing, for seeing much too much again
Prostrate in heat and shivering at dusk
When the time comes... it speaks with abated breath
Time for life and time for –
Roots lost somewhere on another planet
Swearing in the cold of the night
As if words had the power to set him free
He is like you and me – only older and – ?
Wiser for having seen the end
And still recalling the beginning
When the time was nothing but the roots
And flesh was nothing but the time
And there was nothing to search for
Safe what we already had...
Now even sleep does not come
Only dawn-drawn in drops of dew
When the old eyes descry another day
And thank God there was no-one there
To hear what he had had to say
To see what he could not:
A king without a crown – a root without a tree
Who knows... maybe God was he.

The Day You Left Me

Spite in the air, goose-skinned trees
Turning their eyes up and barking back
At this play of tempers, disbeliefs
The early hours, the sunless skies
The gusts of guttered memories
A congregation of seeming lies –
What is this bleakness? This
Lingering and waning? This
Oversized, irresolute child The Day
Of timelessness, growing thin
Of a missed occasion in between
Of the disconnection – call it Sin…?

So it was – between the rainy spells
After making up with the wind
Unraveling a few threads that one tells
One needs to tell, a story to rescind
The monstrous Leap ahead
To calm and sooth one's Heart
While the others sleep in peace…
Not missing any Sun, nor any part
That makes up the whole of Happiness

So it was – on a non-day, waiting
For the Sun to rise again – what bliss
Unmaking Life to see it through
In between the spells of nights
Shivering – without You
Inside my esoteric quilts of rights
Slowly disappearing, in a swoon
Out of sight, from each other's sight
The Day when you left me for the Moon…

Just Enough

Life is too short to wear them out
Life is too long to save them
Life is as it ought to be – long
Just enough for You and Me
Too long for one generation
To wear out their pantaloons
To spare the picture of a youthful face
To pull up the trousers, tie the laces –
Life-like cut across your pate
Like a path from nowhere to
Nowhere – like you
Spelling sunshine mysteries of
Glistening Fates, beatitudes, the bliss…
Then the eye looks aside – a-wrinkle deep
And you wonder why it is so long
Because you cannot sleep at night
And must go on and on and on –
Until another daybreak meets its dawn
Until the pantaloons stay on the hanger
And you whisper: "Life – was kind to me…"
That is the mystery of it all
The pantaloons, the pates, the eyes
That stare at You and say:
It will be OK, I will wear'em out
What you did not do, I can do without.
Sobering years of life
Saving it all – as if this body
This sagging skin and uneasy brow
Needed no more than a barrel –

Some Alexander to spell it out
Some Painter's ear to proudly show
Some Other One to listen, and listen to, and know:
There is so much that one can do without
And so much that One can do
In so little time.

Veni et Vidi

I swear I could do better than that
Be happy-go-lucky and be glad
Be for it all and with one breath
Send it to hell and leave –
Leave behind a bunch of old pals
Memories, mementos mori, gals
Who could not be contented
With a pocketful of hand
Men who could never comprehend
And others who would fend me off
With a disgruntled by-and-by
I will come before I die... so –
By-and-by and would learn too
Know desert and storm and you
Who sit on the sturdiest bough
Peeking though leaves and all
Me – so small – still here
There is something in the air
There is something in the gust to come
Something so near it thrills this soul
I came without a precise goal
And so shall leave – with what?
A pocketful of dust and a knot on the handkerchief
I lived my life, you see,
In joy and without grief or – better still:
I lived without a goal but full of Will.

Eat of My Heart –

Sobering faces strolling by
Grinning and empty-bottomed lovers
Sarte their Idol – dreaming Picasso
Surveilling sunshine, perhaps
Seeing nothing – the stars, the Sun
A ball of empty gas…
Alabaster circles to confuse the mind
Holes through the canvasses of quietude
Each with a halo and a memory –
If the city rats could only speak and see…
If they could only be alive!
Shake their petrified thrill and
Take one word – take any word!
And break it apart –
And eat and eat and eat of it –
Eat of My Heart…

Too old

I wish I could say more of my past than that one thing
I wish I could recall the good times better and the bad forget
I wish I could sing and be glad for forgetting
Be glad for remembering the unremembered yet
Many a mile must be crossed and many a napkin woven
Many a mouth must speak but one – and in a dream
Where passions wake will that one tell the truth
Spell it slowly – like the tears of youth…
She will tell it like a crossed line on the telephone
Stardust grown cold around her mouth, as morrow dew
She will whisper just for you – syllable-by-syllable
A forlorn tale and lonely one, filled with longing…
She will say: "But if you only knew…" and then?
Silent be – stay silent – a minute for her and yourself
Silence – the only healthy thing about hell
And the one pestilential plague in heaven
So She sings – now – a deaf-mute rose – one but one
Among millions of others: too old, she tells me,
Too old to know but one painful memory…
And too young to forget – .

Distant Sounds

Panoply of voices – cacophony of sounds
Let not silences abound – move!
We are all in the groove, baby! – What
Did you think? What do they say?
Nothing. Nothing today. Nothing
Yesterday – the Sun was up and so
The day moved away: a tick, a buzz
We ooze through the pores of the Earth –
Silence returns with dusk. You can trust
Silence. It is the echo of the day
Reverberating in the veins, the echo
Of a lonely crow that nobody can hear:
I lived once. I loved once too. Like you.
Like once was enough… and too much
At times, perhaps, we forget, and then
The cacophony emerges again:
The cackle of the dust. The canter of the vain
That know not of life, the day, but
The airs – aspirations – screams and yells
Exhalations – spells: leaves tremble
Down below I fear…
Once upon a time, a soul did hear
One time – one rhyme – and all will disappear…

Chariots of Destiny

When all our loves have flown away
And nothing seems all right
The night but blended into Day
Shrugs her shoulders in our sight
Last summer's leaves in disarray –
The mirror of our fight
With a crow, by the wall, to say:
"Good-day," perchance, "good-night…"
When this Nature's Course and Lay
Of dust upon a bedside shelf
Of Forces holding us in sway
And lonely hearts bidding health
Latticed lateness of a limpid eye
Lacking the Power to see
From the lynchpin of a lonelier I
Chased on the retinas of Memory
Where is that opulence and wealth
That should give Virtue strength?
Where is that Me in Me Myself
Would make One of all at any length?
The sky shaded – somewhere far away
(Of spaces strange we take a bite)
Supernovas flame and God may pray
Where our Love has flown tonight
Where all our loves had flown do we
Hear the Chariots of Destiny
Whose wheels disturb our silent sea
Of deep Desire – of Darkest Fear
While through the shallows we must steer
And in the most ephemeral see – Eternity.

To Alan

I still remember you: your eyes that like wells of Kindness that would make my Peace
Still accompany me, wherever I go: *What Eyes they were! What Life in that stare!*
There you are with me again – panting and scampering, running around
Chasing chicken across the yard as if there were no tomorrow…
Until even you grew tired, shuffled your mightiness to your wooden shack or
Lay your large head on the porch, and *God Bless You* fell asleep
Your huge ears hanging like Lotus leaves on a Byzantine behemoth
Your big Heart heaving the mass of monstrous energy put to most efficient use
A little powerplant of Happiness, a little more than our human condescension grants
Because we are too full of brains to give way to the floods of Love…
You were the kindest guy I ever knew, always happy for me, You
Happy with a single bone, a touch, a scratch, a dirty grind in the corner
On the lookout, on your vigil, on your watch at all times – watching out for us
Full of concern and care if anything went not the way it should, or not the way
You imagined that it would, not your gracious goodness doggie way…
True, you had your faults too – but, I cannot think of a single one right now
All I can recall is your wolf-like fangs carrying a forlorn piglet to her mummy
Your wagging tail – *Is there anything more cute than a wagging tail?*
Your paws upon my shoulders and your huge tongue all over my face
You see, we are the human race, we do not do that… Why? We should, I say now

And feel like a crazy cow lost in the city searching for a long-lost
friend
It could be a wolf-kind, which you would not recommend, I know but
still
If you were here, I would not have to search at all and would be much
less mad
For being alive, while you cannot be, while you lie dead somewhere
years ago
And there is no-one who will ever know...

The Depths of Human Love

No other thing or creature can
Love as a human being
Be it a child, a woman, or a man
I stand amazed at seeing
The depths of Human Love

The dogs are faithful, but
Their eyes and ears and lips
Keep silent, forever shut
To sacred human pleas
To the depths of Human Love

Cats are fickle in their feeling
Will not come when you call
They seem to be forever fleeing
Their minds and hearts – too small
For the depths of Human Love

A parrot, here and there, will speak
The words that we need to hear
But, out of cage, will seek
The life of a lonely buccaneer
Not the depths of Human Love

Some people have snakes, or even
Lizards or turtles keep
Which is strange, given
That they are cold and never weep
For the depths of Human Love

Because no other creature can
Love as a human being
Long, as a woman for a man
The Man who will keep on trying
To conquer, and to comprehend
      The depths of human love
      The depths of her love.

Now fare thee well at the very last
Fare thee well, sentimental dreams
The past that nailed upon the mast
Invites but monsters' self-esteem

Mon semblable! How I long to be
That rhyme that rises-falls with Thee
How I long to be upon the sea
How I long to face my Destiny!

I have been a sailor many a year
I swallowed pride, yet had my cheer
I have swum and drank my sweat
And undefeated come to Lord as yet!

And all my life has been a dream
A struggle, night-mare, and a whim
A culmination of impossible selves
Dissolved in soil where it still delves

The soil I have walked and prayed upon
To which I am buried now, and gone
Yet, there are those dreams and visions
And cups of silent indecisions

That I leave behind with sentimental dreams
Avast! Away! It all but seems…

To bring me back to that field
Where we can share the golden days
To have me lie alone and yield
Now to the dreams and prayers

The tales of Loves untold!
Those slowly sauntered afternoons!
Forever falling years on hold
Dazzled, puzzled, in a swoon

Longing Loves, passing *Paramours*
Marigolds that toss and turn
Perplexed, afraid of detours

Most shall winnowed weed perceive
None grieve for a tawny flower
But will I rise in joyous grief
Laugh merrily and tower above

I too have seen them – sprightly gnomes
Cheering my Soul in Thee
Smiling upon a cloud high above the sea

When hours still my Mind still roams
Sharing the dreamy mystery
Eyes descend upon the day as we begin to be.

So Much Depends

So much depends
On the yellow submarine
That none of us has ever seen
Hiding by the ocean floor
Singing the old song
Saudis – Iraqis! – so long!
I too have been there before
And am not going back
Not no more
Mum? Say I am done
What is next
Send a message to the Chief
I still believe
I still believe
But I am not fighting, sir
          Not no more!

They always speak of the snows of yesterday
A tear on the cheek and a prolonged smile
They have good teeth and know what to say
And drag you in your dreams and draw a sigh
A breath upon the double-glazing spells it out
Secrets of the silences gone by
Stillness which whispers as it hovers all about
The memories that can never ever die
We all cry even though it seems uncertain
That past has flown to foreign lands
Even though we hate the hurting
And there is no-one understands
We most reveal that which we deem great
Then bend and turn to smell that rose
That srpun

Printed in the United States
By Bookmasters